# Good Enough to Eat

## Brock Cole

FARRAR STRAUS GIROUX
NEW YORK

*For Susan*

Once there was a poor girl who had no mama and no papa and nothing at all, not even a name. So some called her Scraps-and-Smells, and some called her Skin-and-Bones, and some called her Sweets-and-Treats, for that was how she earned her living—selling stale buns and paper birds in the market.

And when she could not get enough
to eat, sometimes she would beg,

and sometimes she would starve,

and sometimes she would put on a straw wig and follow
people in the street, singing:

> My purse is empty, so's my head,
> A sack of straw my house and bed.
> Give me a burden, give me a task.
> A penny, a penny is all that I ask.

Now, the people in the town thought her a pest and a bother. They would have sent her off to live in the woods on acorns and nettles, but the mayor would not have it.

"The poor are always with us, and no good deed goes unrewarded," he said. And wouldn't you know? He turned out to be right.

For an Ogre came knocking at the gate demanding that a fair maiden join him as his bride, or else, he promised, he'd ravage the town. Oh, he was a foul creature! His breath smelled of graves, and he had rats in his hair instead of lice. What could be done?

The mayor called all the girls together and said, "Now, girls, the Ogre wants someone sweet and delectable to be his bride, and I know you all think it should be you, but it would not be fair to choose without a vote first."

And who do you think won?

Well, Scraps-and-Smells had forty-
two votes, and Skin-and-Bones had
thirty-one, and Sweets-and-Treats
had all the rest, except for one that
no one could read because the person
who marked it could not write.

So they dressed the girl in a fine gown and a crown of gold paper to make her beautiful,

and then they put her in a sack so she could not wander off, and then they put her outside the gate for the Ogre.

"Ha! What's this?" said the Ogre, squinting at the sack.
"Scraps-and-Smells," said the girl.

"Scraps and smells? Not good enough!" roared the Ogre. He smashed two crates of chickens with his foot and, reaching over the wall, snatched up:

*A sow and her farrow*
*Scooped up in a barrow,*
*A horse and a sheep,*
*A bull fast asleep.*

And these he swallowed whole.

While he was busy, the townspeople fetched the girl back inside the gate.

"Oh, what does he want?" they cried, wringing their hands. "Not a sweeter, plumper girl! Surely not that."

"Oh, no," said the girl. "He wants me, but he says I must have a dowry, too—a purse full of gold and jewels. And he says it should be a really big one."

"Why, yes, of course. A bride must have a dowry," said the people. So they gathered up all their gold coins and fine jewelry in a purse, put them in the sack with the girl, and carried them together outside the gate for the Ogre.

"What is this?" said the Ogre, snatching up the sack and sniffing at it with his rotten nose.

"Skin-and-Bones!" shouted the girl in a bold voice.

"Skin and bones? NOT GOOD ENOUGH!" shouted the Ogre. He threw the sack back over the wall, and then, reaching into the town, he tore the roof off a house and caught:

Three goats and a hog,
A cow and a dog,
Nine hens, all good layers,
A worthy old dame
Saying her prayers.

And these, too, he swallowed whole.

By the time the townspeople found the girl in a haystack where she'd come down, they were tearing at their hair and shrieking to heaven.

"Oh, what more could he possibly want?" they asked. "We've given him all of our gold and jewels. We've nothing left to give!"

"Ah, but an Ogre's wife must have a sword to cut up his meat," said the girl when she'd caught her breath. "Nothing but a sharp sword will do, and that will be enough."

"Yes, of course," said the people. "She must have a sword to cut up his meat. It isn't good to swallow things whole." So the mayor fetched the sharpest sword he could find, and the townsfolk put sword, purse of gold, and girl all together in the sack and pushed it outside the gate for the Ogre.

Oh, the Ogre had grown bigger than ever with all he had eaten. Big enough to eat the stones of the town walls and use the flagpoles for toothpicks if he wanted.

"What's this?" he roared.

"Sweets-and-Treats!" cried the girl in a loud voice.

"Ah, sweets and treats? GOOD ENOUGH TO EAT!" said the Ogre. And what do you think?

He swallowed up sack, sword, purse, and girl, all in a single bite.

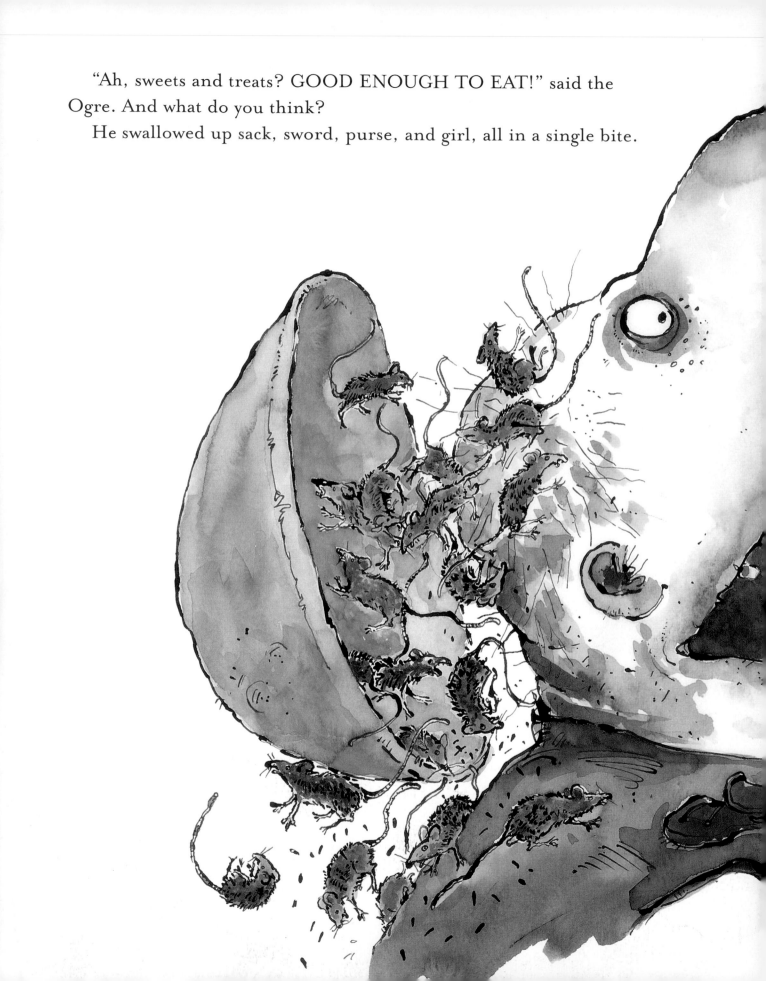

Quick as three winks, the girl took up the sword
and cut once through the sack, once through the
Ogre's black heart, and once through his belly.

Down he fell in a pile of dust and ash, and out
she popped, whole and sound.

When the townspeople saw what had happened, they cheered from the walls and threw open the gates.

"Come in, Scraps-and-Smells! Come in, Skin-and-Bones!" they cried. "And don't forget the purse, Sweets-and-Treats!"

"And what will you give me?" asked the girl.

"A pancake and a sausage!" cried one.

"A sack of oats and a yard of cloth!" cried another.

"Why, a barrel to live in and a new pair of shoes," said the mayor.

A barrel to live in and a new pair of shoes?

"NOT GOOD ENOUGH!" cried the girl. And off she went, down the road in her fine gown with her sword and purse and good company, too, singing:

*I've carried the burden, the task is done.*
*I'll have my penny, and more than one.*
*Should anyone ask who makes the claim,*
*Say Good-Enough-to-Eat's the name!*

Copyright © 2007 by Brock Cole
All rights reserved
Distributed in Canada by Douglas & McIntyre Ltd.
Color separations by Chroma Graphics PTE Ltd.
Printed and bound in China by South China Printing Co. Ltd.
Designed by Robbin Gourley
First edition, 2007
1    3    5    7    9    10    8    6    4    2

www.fsgkidsbooks.com

Library of Congress Cataloging-in-Publication Data
Cole, Brock.
    Good enough to eat / Brock Cole.— 1st ed.
        p.    cm.
    Summary: When an Ogre comes to town demanding a bride, the mayor sacrifices the
homeless girl with no name that everyone thinks of as a pest and bother, but she takes
control of the situation and outwits them all.
    ISBN-13: 978-0-374-32737-8
    ISBN-10: 0-374-32737-8
    [1. Orphans—Fiction.    2. Homeless persons—Fiction.    3. Ghouls and ogres—Fiction.]
I. Title.

PZ7.C67342 Go 2007
[E]—dc22

                                                                        2006037368